The Queen of Mean
The Conversion of a Cold and Prejudiced Heart

Ariele M. Huff

This book is dedicated to all my immigrant and refugee students. Their stories of bravery and misfortunes overcome made me cry; those stories are all in this book which was written in hopes for more compassion flowing both ways between all people who share more similarities than differences. In other words, all of us.

PROLOGUE

"She so mean, she so mean, Bernadine."

"2-4-6-8, who do we really hate? Bern-a-dine, BERNADINE."

...a note in Bernadine's locker said, "I'll get you." That afternoon, after school, there they were. Brigit and her friends...standing across Bernadine's path.

"You're mean," said Brigit and landed a thump on Bernadine's stomach. The girls walked on, laughing. The Queen of Mean had been born and named.

Chapter one

The Queen of Mean, Bernadine. No one actually called her this anymore, but Bernadine would not have been displeased with the label. She might have had it engraved on a brass plaque for her counter, considered it a promotion to be attained if she had ever thought of it. Instead, she just worked toward a general goal that could have been summed up as Queen of Mean. But she wasn't much for introspection or analysis, not much for adding up the likelihoods and improbabilities and assigning them names.

When Lan Nguyen tried to explain her living condition, tried to account for how she could be supporting twelve people in a three-room apartment, Bernadine quite legally refused Lan an extra monthly food voucher: the form only had blanks for number of family members going up to ten individuals. Was it Bernadine's fault no one had considered the remote possibility of a family group of eleven, twelve, or even more?

Her clients, who inspired Bernadine to strive for new heights in pettiness and royal position in cruelty, would have agreed with the sentiment behind Queen of Mean, but didn't possess enough skill in the English language to design such a rhyming tag. They came close to the essence of it in the looks they used amongst themselves and often slightly within Bernadine's view.

That was part of the problem, of course. It wasn't all Bernadine's fault: Her job was difficult, her supervisors uncaring, the resources she was dispensing were limited, and those she was hired to help were needy, demanding, and suspicious.

Bernadine fit their stereotype of the prejudiced, resentful, unfair American bureaucrat.

And, for the most part, they fit, or came to fit, her stereotype of the insistent, pestering, resentful cultural misfit foreigners. In many ways the pattern, the vicious cycle of these stereotypes, was reassuring for both sides. It was a marriage made, if not in heaven, some place where perfect matches can create perfect disharmony. Both sides had comfort in their roles and in the known quality of the other's identity.

Of course, this comfort did not ease the contrast of Bernadine's navy blue office attire, sensible shoes for standing, and close vision specs dangling from her neck on a plastic chain or perched on the bridge of her nose with the ethnic choices of her clientele. Bernadine thought they even wore their American clothes in a foreign way: with a scarf twisted strangely, a cuff turned too far or not far enough, an unusual combination of colors or patterns, a clearly imported accessory.

Even hair styles betrayed the difference, expanded the gap. Bernadine's short, expedient office worker cut feathered her dry, gray hair around her round gold or silver earrings. Her clients sported Ukrainian braids, glossy black straight-cut bangs, Hispanic curls, samurai ponytails, and heads protected from view by scarves and turbans. If Bernadine was a cliché over-worked, irritable, middle-aged administrator, her clients were equally representative of clichés of their own cultures.

Perhaps, it was the continuous stream of foreign clichés that helped to keep Bernadine so firmly in her own niche. Her clients slowly adapted to their new culture: learned English, began to dress and talk as Americans, learned how far to roll their cuffs, what colors not to wear together. Bernadine's clients graduated from the harsh school of Bernadine, the academy of curt replies, rote instructions, and doors slammed on pleading looks. After cruising her sterile halls and punitive classrooms, a diploma in "not so foreign anymore" was imprinted on the immigrants' pupils; you could see it in their eyes: "Bernadine's pupil—graduated."

Bernadine herself stayed in a perpetual state of ungraduatedness. She never assimilated, changed due to the influences surrounding her. She was skotchgarded against any stain of similarity and, therefore, locked ever more tightly into her own navy blue world.

Until the freckle.

Chapter 2

It was exactly September 18th at 6 p.m. when Bernadine noticed it. Not that she hadn't known she had a mole, or freckle, or beauty spot on her upper arm. But on September 18th (her birthday) when she was taking off her green pinstriped shirtwaist blouse, Bernadine caught a glimpse of it in the full-length door mirror. The mole or freckle, located approximately two inches down her upper arm from the edge of an average-size shoulder pad, had definitely changed.

For years Bernadine had grown used to the 1/8th inch diameter midnight dot, but, on September 18th at 6 p.m., her glance was caught and held by the tiny spot. The freckle was clearly at least 1/4 of an inch across: a doubling in size since she had last looked at it, or at least since she had last truly observed it with awareness. Bernadine made a mental note (not without some apprehension) to call for an appointment to have the freckle checked. September the 18th was her fiftieth birthday.

That night on the edge of sleep, drifting midnight blue like her business suits as consciousness folded inward, Bernadine's inner gaze settled on a colorful vision from childhood. Dancing beneath a red and yellow sombrero; castanets or maracas ticking, tickling; fluting hemline undulating and swirling with alternating bands of gold and white: a senorita. A memory

6

from a book? A glimpse from a 1940s movie? No face was visible; just a curl of black hair peeked from beneath the sombrero's edge, around the huge, over-sized brim. Even in sleep, Bernadine pondered: Would women in Mexico really dress this way? Had they ever?

The woman spun close to the lens of Bernadine's interior projector. The brim lifted for only a moment, but imprinting an image: beneath the sombrero, Bernadine's own startled face. She awoke in a chilling sweat.

Chapter 3

On September 21st before calling the doctor, Bernadine pushed up her sweater sleeve to be sure she hadn't been mistaken. To her horror, the spot was now not only one-half inch in diameter, but it was no longer perfectly circular. The edges appeared slightly scalloped with stray irregular streaks, a kind of fringed edge effect. Bernadine requested an emergency appointment and was given it.

On September 22nd, Dr. Cross carefully measured and examined Bernadine's rapidly expanding inhabitant. It had grown to a ¾-inch diameter overnight and was curiously splotchy with some light spots in it. Looking quizzically at the smudge, Dr. Cross declared it was not a mole; there was no protruding flesh. The spot was as flat as tissue paper. Dr. Cross prescribed a topical cream and recommended another appointment in a month with a wait-and-see attitude until then, and a biopsy in the near offing. But no such medical interventions were to be necessary—or of any use.

That night the senorita danced again, furiously clicking the heels of her patent leather pumps. Did they do that in Mexico or only in Spain? Faster and faster, her dress rising like a sun warped record around her rapidly moving knees. Turning, turning. Why didn't she fall down? Bernadine waited for the glimpse of her own face. The sombrero was gone, but the dark, curly head remained amazingly in rear view, even during all the rotations. Toward morning the swiftly tapping feet settled into Bernadine's chest. She awoke to her heart's quickened beat—a sense of anticipation hung in the bedroom air. Bernadine opened a new room freshener, piney and antiseptic.

Chapter 4

September the 25th: Before donning her authority-projecting outfit of the day, Bernadine anxiously checked her upper arm and saw in two-inch diameter, the birth complete, the compilation and composite of so many of the faces she saw each day. Were they the tangled dark curls of Azerbaijani Marina or Hispanic Maria? Were the high cheekbones Gabriella's or Fatima's? The ethnicity was not at all clear, but the gender was definitely female. Bernadine had a face on her arm, not a freckle, or a mole, or even a cancerous tumor. A face.

Bernadine stared, her fingers slowly sliding the perimeter of the image. Perhaps she sought the edge of a scab to lift and relieve herself of the vision. There was none.

Almost before Bernadine's eyes were closed, the dream senorita flashed into view. Her face could clearly be seen, and it was a familiar visage, but it was not Bernadine's. The curls and eyes and laughing mouth and dimpled chin were identical to those now imprinted on Bernadine's skin!

The face floated, floated amongst a revolving array of ethnic costumes. One moment the dark eyes hovered above a shiny pink-edged kimono, the hair slick and geisha-styled. Next the shifting, knowing smile lingered over a French peasant blouse, the hair trained into a thick braid.

Then a fur-lined hood surrounded the high cheekbones; a bulky parka met mittens and leather mukluks.

So many different costumes surrounded the face, fading in and out of each other, mingling, Bernadine felt dizzy. She had the sleep dizziness everyone has felt: the dizziness before falling from the top of a building and awaking with a start, just before reaching the hard, final floor.

The bewildering fashion show continued, and Bernadine remembered her "Dolls of Foreign Lands" paper doll set. In it, too, one form could be wrapped or draped by paper tabs in mixed attire. An inventive child could pair a lacquered Japanese coif with a German dirndl, Mexican serape with Scottish kilt, Basque lace with Guatemalan homespun cotton.

As she dreamed, paper edges flapped and lifted, spread and settled, combined and recombined, finally, flying like birds around and around the face, the unchanging face.

Bernadine could feel the whisper of the feathers fluttering—across her cheek. Her feeling of equilibrium returned, and she awoke quite gently, as though brought safely to earth by multiple, sturdy wings.

Chapter 5

"It's like stigmata, I bet. Or astigmata. Or is that astigmatism? I get those words confused. But one of them means this thing that happens to religious people sometimes when they get wounds or bleed because they're so devout. I heard about one nun who got the picture of Christ on her palm. Sort of like that. Only why would you get this Mexican girl? You aren't even religious. But it's the only thing I can think of. Bizarre, isn't it?" Cherie dabbed at the steamed milk foam mustache she had gotten from her mocha latte.

As Bernadine's co-worker and confidante, Cherie had been shown the inkblot cum portrait A.K.A. line drawing and had been devolving a rational explanation for it all day; although, in her own mind, it was a closed question: Bernadine had flipped out and gotten a tattoo. Perhaps she had been drunk and gotten it. Maybe there was a scurrilous lover or group of unsavory friends who had inflicted the design.

Bernadine's private life had always been very private. She did not intermingle much with her co-workers, at all with her superiors or clients. In fact, she didn't intermingle, intertwine, or interact with anyone. But Cherie was not a good enough friend to know that, and she was not so fond of the Queen of Mean not to presume some dusky secret. After all, there was the stapler incident, and anyone who could refuse a fellow employee a single ridge of staples...well.

Chapter 6

Pavel was Bernadine's last appointment of the day. He sat with pale hands folded, awaiting her decision. His Ukrainian jaw worked slightly as he watched her scratching away at the form in front of her. He couldn't have read the words if they'd been right side up or understood their impact if he could have read them. But he knew these words meant a roof over his family's heads for the next month. A lot can happen in a month. Pavel had been a high-paid architect in his own country, but he had discovered there was little call in the U.S. for an architect who could communicate only in broken English.

"Mr. Podluzny, you missed the first of the month deadline for requesting supplemental housing funds. This means the requisitioned resources have been otherwise distributed prior to your submission." Bernadine leaned over the desk, poking her pencil at various spots on the form.   "This was incorrectly completed. Your birth data is in the incorrect order, and you placed your signature on the line above the desired position. You also only provided your wife's surname, not her maiden name or given name."

Slack-jawed and fumbling fingered, Pavel made his best effort in his uncomfortable second language, "No one help me do this. In my country, day come before month in birth numbers. In my country, we don't give two names always."

Bernadine's lips and eyes went to slits. She'd heard this "in my country" excuse so many times before. It didn't matter that she spent hours and hours every week trying to translate and complete these partially filled out forms. These people who sat before her didn't know and couldn't care less that she was not accorded time to assist them in filling out the forms, that if she handed her superiors incomplete paperwork, Bernadine herself would be treated as though she did not know how they should have been done.

"You'll need to learn how to do things the way we do them in *this* country." She was right, of course, but it meant Pavel would have to borrow from his brother-in-law for another month. He was lucky to have someone from whom he could borrow. Pavel left without looking at Bernadine; he was remembering watching his neighbor being killed in the street for belonging to the wrong political party. In his own language Pavel was thinking, That is why I'm here, and if I can survive that, I can survive this. Pavel was well on his way to graduating from the strict school of Bernadine.

Deeply, deeply Bernadine slept that night. The deeper her sleep, the colder she felt, until crystals of snow were biting at her eyes and lips. Through the chalky flurry came the one Bernadine thought of as the senorita, whirling, whirling. She was dressed this time in fur-edged babushka, muff, thick woolen skirts, and tall red boots. As she swirled by, her arm curved out and scooped Bernadine into her circling, around and around—the dizzy feeling again. And, when it slowed, Bernadine found herself in a room with the snow outside, and all the people inside looked like Pavel: blonde, square-jawed, and pale-skinned. Strangely enough, Bernadine could understand their language.

A grandmotherly person with apron and kindly apple cheeks was telling a story about a witch named Babyaga who had a house on chicken legs and a mischievous cat. Babyaga was an evil woman whose sins included vicious inhospitality to guests. When visitors approached, her house would spin on its chicken legs, disallowing admittance.

The grandmother spoke in disparaging tones, thick with disapproval of this ungracious behavior. At one point, Bernadine was sure the angry gaze settled right upon her, almost sinking into the space between her eyes. "After all," the grandmother continued, "all good Russians are very good to their guests." And she enfolded the grandchildren around her in a demonstration of her national trait.

The next instant, Bernadine felt the dancer's arm about her waist tighten and arc her out of the homey scene. Back in the snow, Bernadine saw the lights of the pleasant home fade, dim, extinguish with distance. In the cold night again, Bernadine felt the chill penetrate her sleep, settle into her bones as the senorita released her and pirouetted a few feet away. She stopped and fixed Bernadine with a steady look, and then she disappeared too. Bernadine was alone and shivering. She wished for the warm kitchen, but knew that she, like Babyaga, had been exiled from it.

Bernadine awoke trembling with the cold and ran to turn up the thermostat. "Winter must be coming," she mumbled to herself.

Chapter 7

The next day, September the 30th, Bernadine found a scribbled note on her desk. It said, "You should gived Pavel temporary short-term aid." At first, Bernadine assumed Pavel had written the note. But if Pavel had known of the temporary short-term aid, wouldn't he have requested it? He would have been well within his rights, and, even though it would have required an extra fifteen minutes to apply, Pavel would, no doubt, have been glad to do that.

Bernadine had thought of this solution as she saw the problems on the form. Had thought of it even before she sat down with Pavel. And, she had known she wouldn't suggest it. Part of her wanted to believe she didn't owe it to him to tell him; he should be responsible for his own needs. And, part of her just didn't want to go to the trouble. Besides, funding was always limited. Who knew when it would be reduced? She received announcements from the government every day warning her that her own job might be eliminated if she didn't find ways to save money. So far, the only way Bernadine had found to save money was to avoid being "overly helpful." She knew the kind of worker who would have made sure Pavel got his temporary aid. Mostly, these staffers were new and idealistic.

Well, there was Shirley down in reception who had been at her job for forty years. Shirley was about to retire, but, in all her years, she'd never turned anyone away because she couldn't understand them or because she was irritated. No one quite knew how Shirley stayed so helpful and cheerful. She was liked by her co-workers too. Shirley didn't turn her challenges into other people's problems. When Than had had a killer toothache, Shirley had called her own dentist and driven Than to the appointment herself. When Lisl was getting married, Shirley told her where to get the license and how to register for wedding gifts. People brought Shirley little gifts: scented wooden earrings from Nairobi, eggrolls, bookmarks gold-engraved with Hungarian proverbs.

No one ever brought anything to Bernadine. Sometimes she was a little afraid to walk out to the parking lot. Bernadine would have suspected Shirley of writing the note but for the language errors that so clearly made it from a foreigner.

During the night, Bernadine dreamed a curtain of flames. In the flames, a familiar face vibrated, bands of light and color forming first an eyebrow, then the edge of the chin, a twisting ringlet, a pulsating pupil, the flickering grin. Bernadine's own hand before her thrust a branding iron into the conflagration, retrieved the dancing visage, and, before her horrified dream eyes, pressed the iron to her upper arm with a sickening sizzling sound.

Awakening in a sweat, Bernadine hustled to turn the thermostat back down. "Indian summer," she muttered.

Chapter 8

Disturbed as she was about the image on her arm, Bernadine still continued to go regularly to work. In October, when she went back to Dr. Cross (after having rigorously, religiously used the skin cream to no effect), he kept his word and biopsied a tiny edge of the senorita, but not until he had closely quizzed Bernadine as to the possibility she had "accidentally" acquired it in some "altered state." The tissue was completely healthy, and Dr. Cross recommended a therapist of his acquaintance.

Chapter 9

The magnifying glass dangled from Dr. Drake's extended fingers, rosary-like, his palm open in an almost supplicant posture.

"It looks like a tattoo," he repeated. "Are you sure there's no time when this could have been done when you were...um...unconscious?"

Bernadine was about to the end of her tether. She had been summarily dismissed by her own doctor who had watched the image grow from a tiny dot to a sizable piece of arm art. She had been told, not asked but told, she could not have gotten this disfigurement any way but externally. She doubted herself and was infuriated. She decided not to tell Dr. Drake about her dreams of the senorita.

"Of course, it can be removed surgically." Dr. Drake seemed to be measuring her reaction and misjudged the anger he saw.

"Wouldn't you like that then?" Maybe she had done this and just had not admitted it fully to herself yet, he thought.

"Whether I have it removed or not doesn't have anything to do with how I got it." Bernadine was using her icy tone, the one designed to send freezing tremors up spines whether Vietnamese, French, Saudi, Costa Rican, or wealthy American psychiatrist. Her icy tone was sort of a universal equalizer, and it worked on Dr. Drake quite effectively.

"Well," lamely, "maybe it's best not to deal with the symptom until we get a better idea of its cause."

The senorita did not show up that night to give her thanks for being spared from the surgeon's laser. Bernadine had almost expected it. Instead, the root of a long forgotten memory sent up a vagrant tendril.

Grizzled and elderly, he was a vagrant. Was his accent Greek, Italian, Hungarian? At five, Bernadine only knew he sounded odd as he tottered toward her, nickel extended between two thickened fingers. He was not like the people she knew.

"Nice-a leetle girl. Here, have a nickole." Bernadine could smell the garlic on his labored breath, could see his cataract-dimmed eyes.

In terror, she ran until she fell over a curb and skinned her knee. The damaged, red-streaked skin, the scraping pain had been his fault. The strange and threatening foreign man had hurt her, and Bernadine would not forget that feeling, even when the event had sifted, like one of many grains of sand, beneath her consciousness for years. The poor old man had been buried in every sense for 45 years but was resurrected in Bernadine's dream, reminding her, "You can never be rid of me."

Chapter 10

October 15th: Get rid of it. Get rid of the senorita? Bernadine hadn't considered the possibility before, hadn't realized it could be done, and, therefore, hadn't had to make the decision. She was surprised not to have a ready answer. The answer should have been clinging to the tip of her tongue, perched on her lower lip, and ready to be pushed into the open air the minute the opportunity presented itself. But it wasn't.

October 15th, night: Bernadine dove from the edge of consciousness into a lava-filled cavern. But, it was not Bernadine of flesh and fears who swam and bobbed in the intense heat. Rather, she was a bit of quartz or metamorphic extrusion, a chunk of granite reabsorbed or sandstone quickly melting. And melt she did. Her absorption was first at one end of the cavern, then on the opposite side, at the bottom of the caldron as a heavy particle, then bubbling to the surface as one of her lighter parts. Bernadine looked for the senorita among the liquid minerals, and, although she found some well-known faces, none of them had the slanted eyes or twinkling smile.

Bernadine was surprised at how comfortable it was percolating in the earth's belly, but when she woke up, a quilt had been thrown to the floor. Truly, the hottest October Bernadine had ever experienced.

Chapter 11

October 16th: Lo Tran spent an hour trying to convince Bernadine to extend transportation benefits to include fuel for a motorcycle, his only method of getting to his minimum wage job.

Bernadine could feel the humid pressure in the pericardium surrounding her heart as the ire rose, strangling her response. Her usual Queen of Mean popsickly composure had been exposed to the August of an internal battle: Part of her knew she could do what Lo wanted, maybe should do it. Another part of her knew the rules, knew she didn't have to do it, knew she was within regulations to deny him. And why not? Bernadine asked herself as she looked at Lo. He was using all his best wiles: trickiness, neediness, pretending not to understand what she was saying, refusing to believe, assuming, assuming, assuming.

Bernadine's dislike and mistrust were regularly filed in the very back of her very last mental drawer. She hadn't taken them out for a good look in a long time, and she now found them intruding in an inconvenient and distracting way.

Lo discovered something was working in his favor; his adversary seemed somehow vulnerable, and he redoubled all his efforts. Bernadine sent the final volley with finality: Period. Get lost. For a moment, they faced each other with raw dislike and mutual consternation.

Bernadine was suddenly and excruciatingly aware of the tattoo that had blossomed on her arm. Covered though it was by a blouse sleeve and the arm of a sweater, Bernadine imagined it glaring a neon welcome to Lo: We are the same. She turned away.

Lo regained his composure. There was more at stake here than motorcycle fuel. Bowing and smiling, he apologized out the door with hope for better luck in later attempts.

The senorita barely waited for sleep to close Bernadine's eyes. She stood angrily, hands on hips, face fully displayed and surrounded by a radiating crown of curls. Her red dress flared defiantly above her wide stance—stamp, stamp—the beginning of a tarantella?

A Vietnamese village flashed into view with huts and fields. Closer, closer as though through a telescopic lens, Bernadine could see inside a hut. Was that Lo Tran squatted in a corner, listening intently? A fire smoldered beneath a boiling pot of long beans. The mother tended the meal while the grandmother told a group of children the story of how chewing the betel seed and areca leaf together had become a marriage custom.

It seems a man had fallen in love with his brother's wife, and when he could no longer stand causing his brother pain this way, he left home. His brother, naturally, followed him out of love, and then the wife, her husband. Each died at the side of the same river; the husband became a betel tree, his wife an areca vine twined amidst his branches, and the brother a white stone at their feet. Their devotion to one another and the suffering each had endured for the others led to the wedding tradition of chewing the leaf and seed together, and then spitting the combination onto the white stone, forming a blood red spot upon it.

The storyteller leaned forward and demonstrated. The man in the corner and the woman tending the pot exchanged a tender look. It was clear; they would search for each other through eternity, if need be, such was their bond.

Again, the angry senorita stepped between Bernadine and the couple; she was tapping her toe and shaking a finger as the dream faded.

Chapter 12

October 17th: Bernadine was covering the lines around her mouth, an exercise in dubious taste and self-delusion, but part of the unvarying preparation ritual with which she fortified herself before the daily onslaught.

As a shell or a wall, it was only paint, but it was thick paint and very concealing.

Bernadine reached for her lipstick and retrieved with it a crumpled piece of paper. Absently, she flattened it. On the memo sheet it said, "Why you so mean to Lo? He a hard worker."

Bernadine was shocked. Had she grabbed the note along with her lipstick at the office or dumped it from a jacket pocket? Certainly, none of her clients had been to her home. There were no other signs of an intruder. And who could have written such a note? Lo would not have referred to himself in third person. Maybe a girlfriend or wife had been told the story, and, like the loyal Vietnamese wife in the dream, had decided to defend her husband. But how could she have gotten the missive to Bernadine so quickly? Lo had been her final client last night.

Bernadine's scalp prickled with fear as she remembered the first note. Was she being stalked and observed by a disgruntled client? It didn't seem impossible.

The thought echoed across the sleep void: It didn't seem impossible.

Bernadine remembered even to her deepest unconsciousness, remembered: She had not been an outgoing little girl, but not shy or easygoing either. "Reserved and unfriendly" were words teachers had used on early report cards. Some teachers had suspected the kind of home that nurtured Bernadine's aloof, snobbish nature: a home where many prejudices were held and expressed with no fear of contradiction. Bernadine had heard, and it phantomed through her sleep mind, "That stupid Brigit O'Toole. Well, what can you expect of a Mick?"

Bernadine had been surprised; she had liked Brigit, her third grade friend. After all, Brigit looked like their kind: quite white and blue-eyed. But Brigit did have that bit of an accent wandering across her tongue, and she did always seem to have trouble understanding the teacher. Okay, so Brigit was stupid and a Mick—whatever that was.

Bernadine found reason to snub the cheery face the next time it approached, to turn her back on the rosy-cheeked girl at lunch, and then again in the art room. Stealing a glimpse from a distance, Bernadine could then see Brigit's downcast eyes and quavering lip. A part of Bernadine felt brave: She was the family's valiant crusader, fighting for all they believed, all that was righteous. A part of her felt the loss of her friend, but, like most children, Bernadine knew how to place her family's wishes over her own.

The next day, a note in Bernadine's locker said, "I'll get you." That afternoon, after school, there they were. Brigit and her friends (true and good and loyal friends) were standing across Bernadine's path.

"You're mean," said Brigit and landed a thump on Bernadine's stomach. The girls walked on, laughing. The Queen of Mean had been born and named. She was a wounded family warrior.

Bernadine awoke in a furious sweat, a sweat of fury. She had been wronged, and she couldn't quite remember by whom.

Chapter 13

All day Bernadine fumed. Her fear had provided fuel for her anger. Instead of being nicer to those she saw, Bernadine was ruder, less fair than usual. She was so brusque, her supervisor, Carol, took notice (and she, herself, was known for brusqueness).

Carol overheard Bernadine tell Chan his English was "abominable." Of course, Carol knew it was true, but you just didn't say things like that to someone's face—not things that could be quoted and could cause trouble for the whole department.

Carol noted the occurrence in her daily calendar. If it came down to it, such an entry could be a useful documentation of her, Carol's, awareness of the problem and intention of dealing with it.

Dreamland: "Bernadine. Oh, Bernadine. Come out and play."

"She so mean, she so mean, Bernadine."

"2-4-6-8, who do we really hate? Bern-a-dine, BERNADINE."

Brigit was a popular little girl; Bernadine had never been, and when the sides divided, everyone was with Brigit, no one with Bernadine. She was a pariah, a patsy, a villainessa. Bernadine: an outcast at eight.

Rather than fading, the memory's hues became more intense as they lingered in unconsciousness. It was as though the film had stopped, and the old-fashioned projector light was searing through the final frame, liquefying the celluloid. Only, no hole was appearing and widening. The colors just brightened, the sound got louder, the rhythm of the chanting increased, the eddying emotions regimented and quickened.

"Who do we *really* hate? BERNADINE."

Chapter 14

October 20th: Mt. Bernadine steamed more every day, releasing an occasional ash plume that floated down over the whole office, drifting from one cubicle to the next. A smell of sulfur suggested an imminent eruption, and, as primitive people often have, the office staff perceived a hellish connection.

Almost every day Bernadine had discovered another note on her desk, at home, in her car, even in her purse or pockets. She was at the boiling point—not the boiling point for blood—the boiling point for steel.

Farhad couldn't have known what he was walking into and was far too proud to care. He believed women were to serve his needs, especially women in this new brash culture, and especially women in what he considered service positions: like administrators of small giveaway programs. His attitude was as imperious and arrogant as Bernadine's had ever been, and he also was angry. Farhad's pregnant wife had been refused medical coupons based on Farhad's new job with his brother-in-law, which placed his as-yet-not-received salary at a level too high to qualify for aid.

Bernadine and Farhad met like two missiles arcing toward opposite targets and stopped prematurely in mid-air. Their mutual but opposed momentum drove them deeply into each other before either of them quite realized what was happening, and, by then, each was splintering, imploding, exploding, and scattering harmful shrapnel in every direction.

Farhad strode up to Bernadine's counter and peremptorily announced that although he had no appointment, he must be seen. He accused Bernadine of discrimination based on his particular ethnicity, and was prepared to launch into a description (filled with recrimination and guilt-producing pathos) of his pregnant wife's current and immediate need for prenatal care and his inability to provide that for the next month.

However, Farhad was met, as was said, mid-air by meteor Bernadine, filled with her own incendiary venom. All the years of unexpressed suspicions fueled the accusations Bernadine targeted at Farhad. He had a great job with good pay. He could afford his wife's medical care, and why should the taxpayers pick up his bills? Why did people come to this country to go on the dole? Why hadn't he, Farhad, stayed in his precious country if he had been so much better treated there?

The concussion and resultant sparks of this collision blessedly obscured some of the specifics from both sides. But the very level of the din well exceeded regulation and brought Carol on the run with several curious onlookers in her wake.

Farhad was removed, soothed, and deposited with another calmer servant of the people, who also told him he was responsible for his doctor bills, but did so in a much nicer way and several decibels more quietly.

Bernadine was promised a meeting with Carol at the end of the day and left to cool her jets in whatever way she was able.

She found she was very little able. Angrily fingering a pen, Bernadine found herself jotting words. With a premonitory chill, she read what her own hand had just written. "When you go learn? You don't listen at anyone. You gone loose your job. Nobody like you...so mean."

The tattoo on Bernadine's arm burned. She jerked up her sleeve to look at it. The girl seemed to be grinning at her.

The dancing began even before Bernadine's head touched the pillow. She had felt it in herself after her barely touched dinner. Robes or skirts had brushed and rubbed by her vital organs as she did the dishes, cleaned her teeth, climbed into bed. Staring wide-eyed and sleepless across her bedroom Bernadine could feel the movement of arms and legs and flowing cloth, and she could hear the insinuating, entrancing music. Lightly, at first, the drums beat time and the flute whispered a tune for the dancers.

Bernadine fought to retain consciousness but saw on her flickering eyelids the dancing girl. The senorita of the tattoo was joined by other dancers. They all wore veils and had long, billowing, dark pajamas covered by long-sleeved tunics. It might only have been clothes dancing but for the occasional glimpse of a henna frescoed ankle or a partial hand, and the ever intensely focussed eyes gleaming above the veil edges.

Into this shifting, turning, swirling group like a rock tossed into the windblown sands strode Farhad in full white Bedouin attire. Even in her sleep Bernadine wondered if Farhad ever had worn such a costume. The dancers sank as one woman to cushions on the floor.

"The She-Ghoul of legend has devoured my child," Farhad intoned. "Ah, Ah-ee," the women moaned and swayed, their draping cloaks swinging like camels' humps on a desert march. "Ah, Ah-eee," it moaned like wind through an empty tent with a thirst no oasis could quench. "Ah, Ah-ee."

"My wife needed a doctor, and the She-Ghoul would not let him come; she perched at the end of the bed and devoured my son as he was brought forth." Farhad turned from the mourners to Bernadine. Closer, closer he came or perhaps enlarged, until his eyes were even with her own, until she thought their foreheads must be touching, until she thought his eyes must be inside her own, until she could read his mind: "She-Ghoul. Hideous She-Ghoul."

Chapter 15

Carol gave Bernadine a one-week suspension for her "burnout."

"It can't happen again" was the baseline.

Bernadine reluctantly called Dr. Drake.

Chapter 16

"Scarification, in one form or another, is part of the rites of passage in many societies. Tattoos, piercing of various body parts, even branding, have often been used throughout the history of the world to signify the transition from one life phase to another: childhood to adolescence, adolescence to adulthood, singleness to the married state, childbirth, promotion in tribal status, inclusion into groups or trades, surviving an illness or injury, menopause...." Dr. Drake paused significantly.

Bernadine remembered an Ethiopian woman whose neck had been ringed with a faded blue picket fence design, clearly homemade. The woman had noticed her gaze. "It hurt," she said with great pride. Many hand gestures and universal facial expressions later, Bernadine knew the woman had been tattooed at age twelve by her aunt and that the tattoo meant Nu had attained womanhood. It had taken all day for the rickety Frankenstein scar to be slowly pricked into her skin around the entire circumference of her neck. It reminded Bernadine of the dog collars some girls liked to wear: a symbol of being possessed, owned, mistreated. To Nu, it was the status and freedom of womanhood.

That night's dream delivered Bernadine to the mouth of a cave, a midnight tunnel. In the backmost recesses something stirred and rustled. A figure rose and came forward. In the dim shadows, Bernadine could see gray hair cascading to the floor. Like smoke, it rippled and surrounded the figure, enveloping her face. Her cloak was stiffly embroidered with Celtic symbols. When she spoke, her voice was somehow familiar, like the echoes in a home where one has lived.

"Three reasons there are in legend for the body to change," the woman chanted. "First," a brittle finger extended toward the cave ceiling, "you can be of magic: a witch or wizard switching bodies as you wish."

"Second," another finger disturbed the stagnant air, "you can be under the spell of such a being. Or," she stepped out of the gloom, "third, you can be born to it, only waiting for the right season to bloom."

She lifted her wrinkled hands and parted the curtain of gray hair. It was Bernadine's face but with an expression so wise and knowing, Bernadine hardly recognized herself at first. She did, however, most thoroughly recognize the face on the shoulder as the old woman's sleeve slid aside to disclose it.

The dizziness swept across Bernadine in a wave. Falling, falling backwards into unconsciousness within unconsciousness. Would the shocks never end?

Chapter 17

Besides seeing Dr. Drake on her enforced week off, Bernadine had decided to use the time getting herself a better car. Hers was on the verge of a metal breakdown and draining off her discretionary funds like the seasoned extortionist it was.

Bernadine had her eye on a nice gray two-door at a lot down the block from her building. The car had only 30,000 miles on it, got good gas mileage, and had no interior or exterior damage. Although it was only two years old, the price was reasonable at $8,000. Bernadine was about ready to buy, but she hoped to negotiate a slightly better price.

On October the 25th, Bernadine went to the dealership first thing in the morning. Start a new day with a new car. Maybe she *would* get that tattoo removed, have a fresh start, be a new woman.

The dealership's owner hustled to meet Bernadine as she posed next to the gray car.

"Can I help?" He polished his hands rapidly together and grinned. He was Middle Eastern. Bernadine knew this meant he was inclined to negotiate and bargain over prices. She turned as though surprised to see a silver Chevrolet behind her.

"Oh, this car. How much are you asking for say...this one?"

Bobbing and hand rubbing, the owner inquired what *she* could pay. Back and forth, Bernadine knew all the tricks of getting the most from someone; she had learned them across her desk from her clientele throughout the years.

"Did you say $8,000? Was that eight? I didn't quite understand. Did you mean seven? Because seven, I can't do seven. But six. Now six, I think...let me look at my checkbook. Six, I think I can manage what with my mother so ill and my husband not working. But, if that's not enough...I'll just keep looking."

They settled on $6,500, a remarkable advantage for Bernadine. She watched the owner scuttle quickly back to his office. He might have been willing to take less, but $6,500 was good, very good.

At first, Bernadine didn't realize how long it was taking for the owner to return. She was looking at herself in the car windows and mirrors, feeling the waxy finish and seat covers, imagining the odometer creeping up as she took trips to rivers and mountains. But, after a while, Bernadine began to glance expectantly toward the office and reception area. She could see the dealership owner in conference with someone else, another Saudi man, probably a partner or employee.

Bernadine's interest meandered back to her car. She planned the new seat covers, car mats, and cup holders she would buy for it. Perhaps she would get a car alarm too.

The owner came hurrying back across the lot. He did not have any papers in his hands.

"I'm sorry. So, so very sorry. This car is already sold. I'm so sorry." His smile and intertwining fingers were as they had been initially, but there was a different temperature in the tone of his voice. Bernadine was startled, stunned as though a basketball had been ricocheted off her forehead. The owner was gesturing and urging her back to her own car, off his lot entirely.

"Well, how about that car?" Bernadine pointed at a red model.

"I'm sorry. So sorry. Sorry, sorry." He continued to herd her out onto the curb. "Have a nice day. I'm sure you find a much better car," he finished as Bernadine hesitantly got into the front seat and swung her legs under the steering wheel.

"Goodbye now." The owner punctuated his final words with a surprisingly hefty shove to the car's door. It slammed with finality. Period. Get lost.

Bernadine watched the car lot owner retreat, no longer scurrying or bobbing; his back was the very picture of resoluteness. In the dealership office, she was almost positive she saw Farhad. Ah, the new job. Bernadine's tattoo grinned at her from beneath her sleeve.

Stepping across the threshold into sleep, Bernadine recalled: "We don't believe in such things." The title of the book in her mother's hands was *Ghosts, Fairies, and Elves.* "We only believe in what you can see with your own eyes," her mother continued.

"We" did not mean Bernadine's parents. It meant her mother and her grandmother and, presumably, all the grandmothers and great-grandmothers before her. It was a kind of matriarchal inheritance, this disbelief in anything unseen or difficult to comprehend. Even in her dream state, Bernadine wondered how her mother would explain the operation of computers. Would she wonder if they were a fantasy, a mass delusion of millions of office workers or a government plot?

Bernadine's mother handed her the book. "Don't check out anymore books like this from the library." And she left the room.

Bernadine could feel the book, feel its faux leather texture in her fourth grader's hand, felt it across the years in her fifty-year-old palm. A premonition shuddered up her arm as her eyes moved in slow motion, down toward the page the book had been opened to: "The Changer Spirit." Across from the story's title in fluttering red and yellow skirts, a rose in her tangling black hair, a lace fan held lightly in her hand, danced the senorita, the girl on Bernadine's arm. It had been their first meeting.

Chapter 18

October the 26th: "Some people believe they can get in touch with other realms through automatic writing, as it is called. The practitioner often goes into a trancelike state and writes furiously. Many of those who do this claim to use different handwriting, to speak in foreign languages, or to report information unknown to them. Modern psychology believes these phenomena are conscious, or sometimes unconscious, acts by the automatic writer." Dr. Drake paused. Bernadine vaguely knew she had been accused of something. Dr. Drake's method seemed to include a lot of innuendo.

"Do you suppose you could get the tattoo to write something here and now?" Dr. Drake's method also seemed to include a certain patronizing tone. Bernadine briefly considered crafting a pseudo-tattoo message, something like "get stuffed, jerk."

"Well, I could try, but the messages always seem to come after something has happened." She shifted uncomfortably. "After a run-in with one of my case load."

"Ah," Dr. Drake said or maybe it was "Aw," but it certainly was not "awe."

"Ah, that is interesting, isn't it? Let's give it a try."

Twenty minutes passed with Bernadine's pen hovering over paper, then resting on the paper. She imagined a plume of steam forming over her own head. She couldn't decide if she was angrier with Dr. Drake for insisting on the test or with the tattoo girl for not performing.

"Perhaps if you started to write something?"

"What shall I write?"

"Why not write about the people in your case load, your clients. This whole tattoo thing seems inextricably bound up with your experience of working with foreigners. Just write how you feel."

Bernadine wrote, "Since I was a little girl, I was afraid of people from other countries. They spoke different languages and looked different. Me too. I saw old movies, and foreign people were usually the enemy: Japanese or Chinese or Germans. They were mostly soldiers and did horrible things to Americans. When I got my job, I was primarily working with poor Americans,

33

but, in the last ten years, I've worked almost entirely with refugees and immigrants. I had no preparation for dealing with language problems or cultural differences. I find people from other cultures are often trying to fool me or get something from me. Me too."

"What do you mean by 'me too' here and here?" Dr. Drake pointed out the parenthetical comments. Bernadine studied the paper. She couldn't recall writing those words. She could make no sense of them. She found herself rubbing her upper arm. It was almost like hugging herself.

Bernadine was not surprised, had gone to sleep expecting the senorita. The smiling eyes and tousled hair were just as in the fairy tale book, just as Bernadine had remembered them and dreamed them. But tonight, the senorita changer spirit, spirit changer was dressed even more familiarly. Her expressive face and exotic hair were perched above an outfit Bernadine recognized from her own closet: a navy blue pinstriped suit with a white man-tailored blouse. Even the silver dome earrings she always wore with the suit were clipped to the senorita's pretty ears.

Somehow, even in this outfit, the senorita scintillated as usual: mischievous, sensual, playful, mercurial. "Who am I?" She didn't say it, but Bernadine could feel her thinking it. Bernadine awoke thinking it, "Who am I?"

Chapter 19

Back at work, Bernadine found herself mildly ineffective, not so angry anymore, kind of numb and not so conscientious in her efforts to control every appointment, dominate every interview. Word was she was going soft. This was not because she did any favors for anyone, but because she was no longer pouring continuous energy into her Queen of Mean status. Like Vesuvius after eruption, she was drained, and she was distracted.

The night before Halloween, Bernadine visited with the gods. Her dreams began as a wall of smoke billowing, gray, sulfury, and dense. From behind the smoke wall, she could hear the clang of hammer on anvil; the hoarse, rushing puff of a bellows. Even Bernadine knew she was in a blacksmith's shop. As the clouds of smoke parted, she saw a swarthy giant with tremendous biceps standing before his forge which was spitting sparks and glowing redly in its heart. Vulcan: another image from a picture book.

As Bernadine watched, she noticed she was within a huge volcanic cone. She could see from inside and from outside, and also below the earth, she discovered. As Vulcan worked at his bellows, the forge grew glowing hot. Beneath the earth, Bernadine could see the bubbling, roiling molten lava pooling and pushing against the restraining ceiling, melting and forcing a path at each surge. The crash of Vulcan's hammer mingled with thunder. The sparks from the forge darted up from the cone like lightning. The anvil shook with Vulcan's blows and the earth trembled.

The boiling basalt streamed upward through every crack and crevice suddenly to burst through, sweeping chunks and boulders into its tumultuous caldron. A gush of energy catapulted the mixture high above the cone's edge, blowing apart the stone walls.

"Stone walls do not a prison make." The words of the famous poem came into Bernadine's mind. She seemed awfully calm, her dream mind pondered, as she watched the fiery maelstrom about her. There, Loki shook the earth in agony as snake's venom stung his face, Poseidon angrily thrashed the waters into tsunami as revenge for losing his throne to Zeus, and Vulcan fanned the flames of his furnace to a white sizzling heat.

The volcano erupted, erupted, blew apart, shook the earth, sent smoke and ash and brimstone scattering, vomited lava until it could vomit no more. The underlying fluid rock was gone; the steam and pressure and heat subsided; the havocking gyration of the earth slackened, lulled, and then ceased altogether.

Bernadine watched calmly as Vulcan set aside his tools for the day. Poseidon, anger spent, retired to his seaweed couch, and Loki's wife Sigyn returned with the blessed cup to catch the serpent's poison. The earth sighed with relief; that was over. In Bernadine's heart, the sigh reverberated, "Ahhh, that's over."

Chapter 20

October 31st, Halloween. Bernadine had been invited to Shirley's Halloween party, as she was every year. For the first time in sixteen years, Bernadine decided to go. Was it because she had been thinking about Shirley a little more lately? Was it because Bernadine was slightly less unpopular with all her co-workers and, therefore, more inclined to socialize? Was it because Bernadine herself was a little more relaxed and sociable in recent weeks?

All of these things were true, but none of them were the real reason Bernadine had decided to go to the Halloween party.

For weeks, she had been thinking about the differences between her looks and the looks of the girl pictured on her arm. A Halloween party seemed a perfect excuse to experiment with this polarity. In fact, Bernadine had not felt free to do this even in the privacy of her own bedroom. Some vestigial superstitious fear, some remnant of possession mythology must have been lodged in a recess of her unconscious (as Dr. Drake would say).

At any rate, All Hallows Eve seemed the safe time to toy with the primitive unconscious, a day when perimeters are temporarily secured around an area normally too risky to explore, a day when nightmares are donned for the purpose of dispelling them.

So Bernadine olived her skin; sculpted her eyebrows; mascara'd her pale lashes; rounded her lips; eye-lined on a slant; pulled a black, curly wig over her sandy hair; and gave herself cheek bones. Before her mirror, she twisted her upper arm under her chin and saw reflected duplicates—large and small, an 8 by 11 and a wallet size.

Selecting an appropriate outfit from her closet was more difficult, actually impossible. Whatever outfit Bernadine tried on made her seem like a combination disembodied senorita/headless office worker. Settling temporarily for a black cotton shift with gold hoop earrings, a wide belt with a gold buckle, and black high heeled pumps, Bernadine headed for *Glad Rags*, a clothing shop located a few blocks from her apartment. She had in mind a peasant blouse and colored circle skirt as the perfect costume to complete her look.

Three other customers were milling around the small boutique when Bernadine arrived. Two of them were her neighbors, and she curiously watched them for signs of recognition. After a few attempts at getting their attention, Bernadine gave up; the women seemed to be avoiding looking at her. The clerk, an acquaintance for years, would be the real test.

Bernadine moved quickly to the blouse section at the back of the store and began enthusiastically "hanger thwacking," searching through the racks of clothes by energetically shoving each item tightly against the last. So involved was she in hunting for the exact puffy sleeves that when the clerk, Jeanette, came and stood behind her, Bernadine jumped, was quite startled. And, during the moment of re-composing herself, she missed the opportunity to speak first, giving Jeanette a voice clue as to her identity.

Whether Bernadine had been more involved in clothes hunting than usual, or whether Jeanette had been stealthier in her approach, the upshot was that Jeanette spoke first, while Bernadine's hand was still fluttering to her chest and her painted eyes were still widened in surprise.

"Can I help you?" Jeanette's voice—could Bernadine be wrong?—sounded arctic compared to her usual heated-honey, please-buy-my-clothes voice.

"The fitting room is being repaired right now so you can purchase that article of clothing, but I'm afraid you won't be able to try it first." Without waiting for an answer or response, Jeanette's back presented itself, and she withdrew to an incommunicative distance from which she posted a close watch...a fixed stare...a police-state vigil.

Bernadine suddenly imagined herself in the act of stealing the blouse, and her hands flew away from it, not quite over her head, and she did not spread her feet or lean against a wall, but, all at once, she knew how that felt.

It became incredibly important to Bernadine's comfort to abandon her search and flee with rapidness, which she did. The other customers stood between her and release, necessitating a head-lowered charge and furtive glance to find the doorway. The glance was furtive but adequate to reveal the unmoving stares of the four women. Did their eyes hiss "Ssspick" or "Fffflip," "Jap" or "Chink?"

Bernadine burst into the clean, clear, smoggy air. She had been mistaken; her costume was complete and perfect as it was.

Chapter 21

At home, Bernadine stripped off the wig and make-up, watching the unchanging tattoo girl as she did. The lipstick came off, the eye shadow rinsed down the drain, the wig frisbeed across the room; it all came off and left her...still fifty years old and still a woman. But, at least not foreign.

Into the mirror, Bernadine stared, no longer at duplicate faces on arm and above it, more like photo reverses.

She sat down at her dressing table, held a pen, and set the point on a piece of paper.

"Who are you?" she said to her arm. Her hand began to move and letters to form.

"Who you want?" And then, "Give me name."

Bernadine had assumed the girl was a complete and developed entity, having some history and identity outside her connection to her hostess, the owner of the arm. The possibility the image had no name before her appearance had never occurred to Bernadine: What kind of virgin birth could this be?

To her arm, Bernadine said, "Brigit," the name of her abandoned third grade friend. Bernadine felt a chuckle resonate along her trapezium and vibrate her triceps and biceps. On paper, "Okay."

Let's get this ethnicity thing cleared up, thought Bernadine.

"Where are you from?" On the paper, "You."

From Bernadine? White Anglo-Saxon Bernadine with grandparents and ancestors as far back as could be found with last names like Wilson, Davis, Harris? From Bernadine whose family albums showed pale faces over Victorian collars, under Missouri straw hats, staring past the flaps of a covered wagon?

But, somehow, Bernadine felt it was true. A warm geyser of maternal pride gurgled up from somewhere within her, a pleasant and small eruption.

That night Brigit and Brigit came hand in hand. Brigit was still a third grade girl with curly copper hair and red cheeks. She and senorita Brigit were both dressed in old-fashioned Irish peasant costumes with bare feet and shawls over their heads.

In a small turf-roofed cottage, Brigit the younger gathered a group of children about her and told the story of a changeling, a human who had been replaced by a fairy. The changeling roused a ruckus and caused no end of trouble until right-thinking friends threatened it with hot pokers from the fire. At that, the changeling fled, leaving a much nicer acting human in its place.

Bernadine thought changelings might just be a metaphor for people who were misbehaving. She decided it was likely the Brigits thought she had been a changeling. But, she was not that anymore...not after the eruption and Halloween and Farhad and Dr. Drake and the Brigits.

Chapter 22

November 1st: Back at work, Bernadine was no longer numb and staring, like a prisoner locked in her own head with her nose pressed up against the interior pane of her eyes. The windows had been flung open, the panes removed, and Bernadine was sitting on the sill, legs dangling in a friendly manner. Everyone began to notice the new Bernadine, the more relaxed, more cooperative, more accessible Bernadine.

Co-workers offered her a cookie if they had cookies to share; Cherie went to lunch with her almost every day and asked Bernadine why she looked younger; Carol stopped by to smile and say good morning; clients began to tell Bernadine the names of their children and show her photos. She accepted these signs of friendship and was pleased.

Lorena, a Costa Rican woman of about fifty, had been added to Bernadine's caseload. She differed from many of the people applying to the program in two significant ways. Lorena had lived in the U.S. for ten years as a citizen, and she had developed a fairly functional ability in English during that time. Her English was accented and grammatically incorrect but showed it had been learned through daily exchanges and by hearing common usage.

Lorena had the idioms, the vocabulary, the syntax to ask on which aisle the tomato soup was kept, to tell a stranger (if asked) that the number five bus goes across town, to order a hamburger without onions, and to complain about an overcharge on her bank account.

Lorena did not have adequate ability with the English language to help her ten-year-old son with his homework, to do her own taxes, or to argue effectively with her native English-speaking husband. In spite of those limitations, Lorena was an abundantly pleasant and communicative woman. She liked to tell everyone how she was going to open her own beauty salon after she finished beauty school. She told Bernadine that she (Bernadine) had a heart-shaped face and would look really fabulous with a permanent. Lorena said, "really faboolus."

Whenever Lorena got an unexpected answer to a question she had asked, she said, "Reeeeely?" drawing out the internal vowel sound in proportion to her incredulity at not getting what she wanted. Lorena was always surprised when life gave her anything but what she wanted, and she rebounded from such surprises by re-categorizing the experiences as "berry goot" lessons for her. Bernadine thought that if she herself were in a new and different culture, she would want to be as resilient and resourceful as Lorena.

Lorena had come to Bernadine's agency to get partial aid for her schooling. After that was accomplished, she began to come in for assistance with other small problems: filling in applications, translating complicated instructions, interpreting difficult textbook paragraphs.

These tasks were clearly outside Bernadine's job description, but they never took long, and Bernadine began to enjoy the productive feeling of helping Lorena achieve her goal. Of Lorena, Brigit said, "She is nice lady—plump and funny."

Drowsing and then pacing backward through a hallway, Bernadine could feel herself getting younger. As she looked at the walls of her hallway, she noticed photographs, pictures, and mementos from her life. Some of the pictures seemed to be active, like movies. As she moved backwards, she became younger and younger in the pictures.

At five, Bernadine stopped and moved closer to an image. The snow was lightly drifting down, and she could see herself watching it from her grandmother's warm parlor windows. Up the sidewalk, slow and halting, came the blind Japanese man with an armload of holly wreathes.

"Grandma, grandma. He's here. Misaaki is here."

Together, little Bernadine and her grandmother threw open the door, helped Misaaki shed his prickly burden on the porch, and drew him inside to warm his hands at the fire and have a cup of tea.

Misaaki held the cup gently in one hand and the saucer in the other. Bernadine had never seen anyone drink tea so delicately, so elegantly, so thoughtfully.

"This is not like tea in my country, but it is very good." He spoke as carefully as he drank tea, and when he said "very," it only sounded a little bit like "velly."

Back in the hallway, still pacing backwards, Bernadine stopped at a picture from her fourth year of life. A tidy farmhouse was surrounded by a neatly kept chicken house, duck pond, and sheep pasture. Inside the home, little Bernadine was visiting Laura and Andy, an elderly Swedish couple. Andy had worked with Bernadine's father until retirement to the little Swedish style farm.

Laura always cooked special foods for Bernadine that had strange names like Rumegrot and Sandbakkel. Bernadine liked everything except the head cheese.

Andy held her on his knee and said, "Vell, vell, vat a big girl." Bernadine loved to go to Laura and Andy's little farm.

Back in the hallway, pacing backwards, Bernadine stopped again at age three. She was watching a group of several Moslem women walk by her. They were swathed from head to toe in veils and skirts, and their clothes wafted exotic, spicy smells. Bernadine was entranced with the tiny hands, feet, and sparkling eyes that seemed to dart out of these piles of clothing. She clapped her hands in delight, and the women, noticing her, chuckled softly and called to her in their own language.

Back in the hallway, Bernadine thought, there were good memories of foreign people, too. She was very pleased to find them. She woke up smiling.

Chapter 23

November 15th: Bernadine went to Lorena's house for a permanent. A chair surrounded by newspapers had been set up in the kitchen next to the large white Formica table, which held bowls, sponges, curlers, and potent, pungent fluids. Potent, but Lorena assured Bernadine, "Permanents chould be berry gentle" for gray hair.

Lorena ruffled and divided Bernadine's pigeon-shaded locks, soaked them in odoriferous solutions, and rolled them in spongy pink curlers. An hour later, Bernadine emerged with soft, shiny clusters of curls, more like dove wings than pigeon pin feathers. Lorena sighed with satisfaction and suggested cranberry colored lipstick, aqua eyeliner, mauve clothing.

Bernadine went home by way of the drugstore (for garnet lip pencil, crimson lip gloss, and turquoise eye liner). In front of her mirror, she experimented with her face and admired the fluffy froth of her new hairdo.

She took out her pad and pencil. Of late, Bernadine had been having regular conversations with Brigit and could often tell when Brigit had something she wanted to say.

"You look good. Like poodle." Bernadine laughed. She had discovered Brigit had a wicked sense of humor, which was often targeted at Bernadine's more straight-laced attitudes and habits.

"It's not as curly as yours," Bernadine retorted without hesitation. On the paper, "Mine not stink."

Bernadine knew how to deal with this. "You stink," she said, laying aside the pencil and tossing a smugly triumphant look to her shoulder. This would be a short-lived victory, of course. Brigit had her methods of revenge: mischievous addendums to Bernadine's memos, inappropriate extras on application forms. It was an ongoing, friendly sparring match and quite amusing to them both, if somewhat embarrassing on occasion—which was part of the amusement too.

Brigit met Bernadine on the edge of her dream with an outstretched hand and an ear-to-ear grin. She pulled her into the same whirling step she'd used many times in past dreams to bring Bernadine into the dance. The undulations got wider and wider until Bernadine could see they were circumnavigating the earth. Like joined snowflakes, they were blown high into the atmosphere above the planet and then close to the earth where they could see Cossack dancers stamp-squatting vigorously to a rapid beating tune.

Back up into the starry night Brigit and Bernadine twirled, pirouetted, and descended in Cambodia where girls with delicate fingers postured with tiny clinking cymbals. Up they went again into the sealskin sky and back down to England where Morris dancers leapt and waved scarves at an exhibition of medieval entertainment.

Up into the glittering sky, making wide turns like space ships in slow motion, skirts billowing and ballooning went Bernadine and Brigit. Back down they came and circled a western line dance with swaying jeans and stomping tooled leather boots. Into the night air the world travelers went, spiraling down in time for a lively German polka, and again up and down for a hibiscus-scented display of the graceful hula. As the night ended, so did the waltz of Bernadine and Brigit. Deposited back into a warm, deep sleep, Bernadine thought of all the happy, celebrating people she had seen that night: a world filled with joyful moments.

Chapter 24

Thanksgiving: Shirley and Bernadine had set four foldout tables down the center of Shirley's long living room. Every year for the last ten years, Shirley had invited fifteen to twenty immigrants and refugees to join her family in their Thanksgiving celebration.

"It's one of the loveliest parts of American culture, and I enjoy sharing it with those who haven't experienced it," she had explained to Bernadine when presenting her with an invitation to come and help.

"Every year we have more people, and I can't handle it by myself anymore." Shirley didn't say she knew Bernadine would be alone, had been alone every holiday for years. Her Thanksgiving parties were not just a time to share her American culture but were also a time when she learned more about her guests' cultures than she did all year long at her reception desk where she dealt with over a hundred people every week. This year—for the first time, Bernadine seemed both interested in and worthy of inclusion.

The tables groaned with food contributions from everyone: turkey and dressing snuggled between humus with pita bread and eggrolls; couscous and peanut sauce shared a tablecloth with a huge pan of spankopita; tamales and hombow circled a plate of sushi with umeboshi plums. Bernadine's pecan/pumpkin double-decker strata pie was side-by-side with baklava and apple strudel.

Dinner was a tower of Babel affair. Bernadine sat between Ivetta and Misbah. She learned at least five different ways to say "pass the gravy." She learned there are many ways to wrap a sari, that the Black Sea is in the Ukraine, and that meals have many courses in Moscow.

While stomach space for dessert was developing, the general conversation turned to reasons for being thankful. One after another the group took the floor to share reasons for gratitude. Lin was grateful her family was still alive in spite of the attack by pirates as their boat made its way to freedom. At twelve, Lin had been raped and had watched as others were raped, robbed, and killed.

Vasiley was appreciative he no longer was the object of persecution based on his black curly hair, dark eyes, and porcelain white skin. In his country, he had run from beatings by vigilante groups more than one time.

Joyce Chan was glad she was making enough money to send back home to support an uncle in prison. She said it took every extra cent to bribe guards to feed and not to beat her relative.

Mahmoda was thankful for an opportunity to go to school. In her country, women were seldom even taught to read. She could not read in her native tongue.

Then it was Bernadine's turn. What could she say? The other stories made her white hot aware of her reasons to be grateful, but where was her pain that could be compared to these harrowing stories? As she looked from one waiting face to the next, it dawned on Bernadine with the glare of a noonday sun erupting over the eastern horizon. Her pain, her loneliness, was clear, but not to be admitted...not then, not there.

In consternation, Bernadine began to drop tears, and once the storm cloud was seeded, it burst. A bouquet of culturally appropriate responses hovered around, across, and over her: Asians averted their eyes and bowed their heads in silent empathy; Hispanics and Russians laid hands and arms on her; a Norwegian slapped her heartily on the back as though Heimliching the sobs right out of her would work. A shower of foreign expressions of sympathy cascaded over Bernadine's head and washed through her like a soothing rain, coated her like a lava flow of love.

The pitter patter of hands stroked and brushed against Brigit beneath Bernadine's cardigan sleeve, and then they, or she, decided it was time to get closer. The sleeve drooped and slid to the elbow. One by one the clutch of comforters spied the arm and fell back into a circle of gawkers. Only a few of their cultures approved of such body art, on women. Nor were they used to seeing American women of Bernadine's kind decorated in such an elaborate way.

"Well," Lorena gave her best full-throated importance to the vowel, "you are a craysee girl." Admiration vibrated through her voice and shone from her biased eyes. She extended a finger and poked Brigit in the nose, causing her to take on a wry and puckered expression.

"I like it velly much," Setsuko intoned gravely. "Very much, very nice," repeated several voices politely.

It might have been Misbah who started the tittering or Joyce who was suppressing a grin behind her hand, and it certainly was Ivetta who began belly laughing and Vasiley who joined her, followed quickly by Maria and Thanh. At any rate, it was probably not Shirley who started it, but everyone, including Bernadine finished it.

Bernadine sank into sleep like a pebble thrown into soft snow. She found herself gazing into the mysterious, crystalline interior of a glacier's snout. A glacial pool reflected the white and blue-edged mass behind it, and cool purple mountains rose into the sky on every side. While Bernadine looked, a light snow began to drift around her, icing the top of the glacier. This is me, Bernadine thought. This is like the way I've been for years: so cold and so lonely. This is like me.

Immediately, a wind surged into the stillness, and Bernadine was blown and swept into a forest where a drenching rain was falling. Lightning and thunder crashed and flickered. A tree nearby was split and blackened to the undergrowth. The rain pelted mercilessly. No, this is me, Bernadine thought. This is like the confusion and upsetting feelings I've been having for months: the confrontations and angry outbursts.

As soon as she thought it, the rain slacked and diminished, and Bernadine found herself looking at a shimmering double rainbow, its ends overlapping. As she continued to watch, the sun brightened, and Bernadine could feel its warmth on her back and head. She felt herself crying with joy and relief. No, this is me, she thought. This is me now: generous and kind, with friends for conversation and companionship. This is me now.

The warmth of the sun penetrated her, and Bernadine awoke feeling relaxed and happy.

Chapter 25

December 1st: Bernadine had just finished explaining to Wen which hand gestures are unacceptable in the U.S. The flush was still in her cheeks (and on his too) when Carol came to invite her to go Christmas shopping.

They took downtown by storm: giggled their way through the Wig Boutique, shuffled the next year's calendars at a stationery store, and traded repartee with the perfume girls in a posh department store. In the hat department, Bernadine glimpsed herself with new silvery, curly locks, aqua-lined eyes, flattering plum silk blouse. She looked better than she'd looked in years; she looked happy. On second look, it really wasn't the blouse, the hair style, or the make-up. It was more the twinkling light sparkling from her eyes to her smile, across her cheeks, over her brow.

In thanks, Bernadine patted Brigit who seemed suffused and lighter herself.

Bernadine and Brigit danced with Christmases past that night. It had been years since Bernadine had remembered her childhood Christmases, remembered why she used to treasure and look forward to this time of year. Years of loneliness and hard work had dimmed the shiny ornaments of yesteryear, had muted the street carolers she now recalled so vividly, had even overpowered the cinnamon and pine tree scents that had always meant Christmas to little Bernadine.

Brigit and Bernadine visited one Christmas after another. The gingerbread and feathery balsam branches, the holly and candles and visiting relatives, and turkey dinners, and Christmas carols: How could she have forgotten all this?

As she wondered, Bernadine was taken to the Christmas when she was twenty-five years old. Both her parents were gone; no other relatives remained. She sat alone at her office desk, working to keep her mind off her problems. Tears did not fall on the typewriter keys, but, as Bernadine watched her young self, she knew there were tears freezing inside her while she labored that long Christmas night.

Twenty-six, twenty-seven, thirty, thirty-five, forty, forty-five, forty-nine: all the adult Christmases looked like one another. Bernadine, aging but still working, still alone. It was a compassionate Brigit who put her arm around Bernadine and drew her back to unconsciousness.

Chapter 26

December 15th: At work, the intuitive grapevine—that information network not requiring direct verbalization, feelings and concepts which hang in the air and are retrieved by passing nervous systems—the intuitive grapevine brought to Bernadine's desk an increasing number of clients. And, increasingly, these people were sharing their lives with her. So many "family photos" had overflowed her cubicle walls that she had created the "friend's fotos" bulletin board in the reception area. So many invitations had blown her way, Bernadine had forgotten what her loneliness had felt like. (Or, perhaps, not forgotten, but remembered thankfully in the past tense.)

In the last month, she had learned of a panoply of winter celebrations: the important New Year festivals in Japan and Vietnam, the 39 Ukrainian fasting days, Svalty Mikulus Day in Czechoslovakia, Swedish St. Lucy's Day, Italian Novena, Badnjak in Yugoslavia, the feast of Epiphany from Brazil, St. Sylvester's Day (Polish), Syrian ceremonies for St. Barbara's Day, English Boxing Day, Dutch Sint Niklass Avond, Hanukkah, and Finnish traditions for St. Stephen's Day.

She learned Mexican homes are usually decorated by the 16th of December, and that in Puerto Rico, January 6th through the 8th are "open house" days. Bernadine was told Armenian Christmas was on either January the 6th or on the 18th, which accords with the Julian calendar. She was told that in Italy January first is the celebration of "twelfth night."

In fact, Bernadine and Brigit (now prominently displayed in sleeveless party dresses) had become central figures in so many homes, they (well, Bernadine) had eaten so many different glazed and frosted and baked and fried holiday specialties, had been exposed to so many flashing and glittering and shimmering ornaments and decorations that they both glowed with the holiday spirit. Brigit seemed stretched like thin black lace over Bernadine's smoothly satisfied arm skin, expanding her grinning smile and her smiling eyes.

The dream started as total happiness, a feeling of content and satisfaction that Bernadine had never known. Was she a fat, purring cat, being patted and stroked? A sunflower, waving in the hot, breezeless August air? Or maybe she was a glowing sunbeam, descending through a raindrop to split prismatically into rainbow colors. It was a delightful feeling, and, when Brigit intruded, Bernadine was not really pleased to see her.

Bernadine was especially not pleased to see her because Brigit was wearing an uncharacteristically serious look on her face. Bernadine felt like a child dragged from a warm bed to go to school. She wanted to stay in the cozy dream she was having. But Brigit was adamant and swinging Bernadine onto her arm, snatched her from her reveries.

And, it was not to pleasant places Brigit wanted to go. The images were painful, sometimes even terrifying: Farhad and his family crouching in a bunker as missiles screamed over their heads, Marina running from a group of ethnic cleansers, Pavel watching his neighbor shot and killed, Lin in a small boat with twenty other hungry people attacked by pirates, Lo escaping under barbed wire, Wen watching a classmate crushed beneath a tank, Vasiley in Russia being beaten for his dark hair and white skin.

Then there were images in the U.S.A.: Lidiya trying to find her father through the State Department, Loan being laughed at in a restaurant for the way she used a fork, Keiko being given the wrong change in a taxi, Hui-Chen being bullied by her landlord, Peter from Nigeria being beaten for his black skin.

Scene after scene of violence, polarity, racism, and discrimination were visited by Bernadine and Brigit. Worst of all, the people being hurt were all known to Bernadine; many of them were friends. She felt limply helpless as she watched and finally turned away and towards Brigit. The two had never spoken before in dreams, only in notes written through Bernadine's hand.

"What can I do? What can I do?" Bernadine said.
"You can help" was the reply.

Chapter 27

Since Bernadine had become more and more included in her clients' lives, she began to hear wisps of rumor, strands of gossip, then outright accusations of discrimination.

Vinh had worked for three years at a moderate paying job when a new worker, an American, was placed under his tutelage. Vinh trained the new man to the best of his ability for a month, and then was stunned when the newcomer was given an immediate promotion and became Vinh's supervisor with a hefty salary and authority over twenty workers.

Vinh's seniority, education, and job performance all suggested he should have been given the supervisory position.

Bernadine recommended a lawsuit, but Vinh was afraid of losing his income and preferred to swallow his pride and his anger, continuing as the subordinate of the man he had trained.

Mai was struggling through college and managing to maintain a 4.0 grade point average when she had the misfortune of taking Clay David's history class. Tearfully, Mai described to Bernadine Professor David's prejudiced comments about the foreign students and their abilities. By mid-quarter, all the non-native English speakers, except Mai, had dropped the class.

Bernadine felt her anger rise as she scanned the homework requirements for the class. Even to her untrained eye, it was clear the curriculum was designed to favor English as first language speakers. Bernadine helped Mai the best she could by reading through her work and looking for missing or extra articles (the, a, an): a common problem for learners of English as a second language and one that is not easily overcome since, she discovered, a standardized rule for all uses does not exist.

Daniella had been in a car accident and was totally lost in all the paperwork and bureaucratic red tape. Although she had been found not-at-fault, Daniella was having great difficulty getting her injuries covered. She shared with Bernadine that when she went to see the two adjusters, they had spoken rapidly, using technical terms and had laughingly imitated her accent within her hearing. Bernadine remembered guiltily her own strategy—could it have been only three months ago?—of ridding herself of demanding clients by speaking confusingly and quickly, and by using complex vocabulary.

Bernadine helped Daniella complete some forms and sent her to a free legal clinic for advice.

Brigit and Bernadine often discussed discrimination in their notes. Initially, Bernadine's anger at the injustices made her ashamed of her own race, country, and previous behavior, but Brigit had a more international perspective.

"There been good, kind people in all places and bad peoples too. Every country have prejudice. It just from two different group." Bernadine knew Brigit meant "between" instead of "from." She had come to interpret Brigit's language mistakes quite easily. Although she had worked with immigrants and refugees for years, it had only been in the past three months that Bernadine had actually been listening and trying to understand, instead of putting her effort into feeling angry because her clients couldn't express themselves more perfectly in English.

Bernadine now discovered she could almost always understand what was being said to her, and she even found the accents and grammatical alterations interesting. It must be admitted those she dealt with were also spending more time and effort trying to be understood by Bernadine. Her new, accessible attitude and reputation were bringing Bernadine a downpour of favors and subtly more favorable conditions.

Some of it was not that subtle. There were wide smiles, thank yous expressed in choked voices, pats and bows, scarves and cards, a flower, a bowl of soup, a hug, an occasional and shy "I like you." Above and beyond these appreciations, Bernadine cherished the shimmer of trust in an eye, the vulnerability of a private secret revealed, the closeness of shared tears, the sense of accomplishment when a client met a goal with her help.

Bernadine was filled and injected with and surrounded by a net of loving energy, and it showed. It showed in her step, in her skin, in her posture, in her voice, especially in her voice which had been caustic and harsh and was now softened and lighter. In every way, Bernadine was lighter. And so was Brigit...noticeably.

Bernadine's dreams now were of light. One night found Brigit and Bernadine circling the moon, filled with the glow until, like shimmering, transparent bubbles, they burst and misted to earth. Another night, Bernadine dreamed she stood beneath a rushing, shining waterfall. As it coursed over her, it began to flow through her. It felt like a bright current, leaving her hollow and peaceful.

Yet another night, Bernadine floated on a white cloud with the sun smiling down on her. She felt herself being saturated with golden warmth. One time, she visited a huge glass palace filled with elaborate chandeliers. She slid up into the crystals, gazed from facet to facet as they refracted and reflected. Afterwards, she felt sparkly all through her body for days, as though she'd drunk liquid quartz or had her interior decorated in diamonds.

Sometimes Bernadine had many dreams of light each night: gliding from candle glow to ruddy hearthside, from lightning flash to Aurora Borealis, from pink dawn to alabaster sunset.

All her dreams were of light.

Chapter 28

December 20th: Carol summoned Bernadine to her office, which was pretty unusual as the two had been lunch and shopping buddies for the last month.

"They've been noticing you upstairs," Carol winked at her. "We want you to head that new department we've been discussing, the acculturation department. You've been doing so much of that kind of activity already; it seemed a natural transition. You seemed the obvious choice. How do you like that, kiddo?" Carol leaned across her desk and gave Bernadine a pat on her Brigit shoulder.

Bernadine's recent transfiguration had re-vitalized Carol, too, rejuvenated her belief in people, excited her enthusiasm for the new project.

"You'll be in charge of a ten-person department to start. We'll want you to design and lead workshops on cultural issues as well as legal, financial, and language problems. It's great, isn't it? Congratulations."

"Merci, Dom Arigato, Graci." Bernadine smilingly voiced the words of thanks so often said to her recently.

After work that evening, Brigit's note said, "You make one difference, it change the whole life. I am glad for you. I think this is best for you too." Bernadine agreed.

That night, Brigit arrived all in rawhide attire. Her long soft dress had fringes around the hemline, neck, and sleeves. On her feet were beaded moccasins and in her curly, dark hair was a brightly colored headband with feathers. She held out her hand to Bernadine, and they traveled far away and long ago to a village of buffalo hide tents gathered in a circle around a huge bonfire. Each tent had special markings on it: circles, crescents, stars, arrows, squares, zigzags.

Men, women, and children warmed themselves around the bonfire as an old woman wove a weaving tale: Time began because an old woman (older than time) began to weave a blanket, using dyed porcupine quills as beads. Each time she leaves her weaving to check the fire or pick berries, her dog pulls out some of the quills. If she ever finishes her blanket, time too will be done. In their turn, each person born is weaving his or her own blanket; some take longer than others. But when the last porcupine quill is woven into the beautiful pattern, the blanket is complete. That is death: when the pattern is completed and the lovely blanket is done. People who know this secret make the very fanciest blankets with the most intricate patterns, because it delays death the longest time possible.

The old woman's eyes seemed to be looking directly into Bernadine's as she said, "May your blanket be the most gorgeous the world has ever seen." And Brigit seemed to whisper, "Good night, Bernadine." The campfire dimmed and went dark.

Chapter 29

December 23rd: The last day of work before the holiday break, and Bernadine was cleaning out her desk to start her new job after the first. Lunch was a Christmas office party, and the only appointments of the day had been completed.

Bernadine slipped out to use the restroom. She returned to a warming sight. On her desk was a lovely, large arrangement of pink chrysanthemums and red carnations with white specks of baby's breath exploding around the edges. The whole thing was held in a white porcelain basket.

Bernadine was charmed, enchanted. Who could it be?

She opened the card, and it said only, "Feliz Navidad, Brigit."

Brigit? How? Where could she...? Bernadine pulled her blouse sleeve up just in time to see the last faint traces of Brigit evaporate. Bernadine was sure she saw Brigit wink as she disappeared, and, floating in the air, the words, "I'll see you in your dreams."

END

Web site: http://ariele.freeservers.com/
Blog: http://fiftyshadesofgraying.blogspot.com/ Send poems, stories, essays for the next eBook.
Website segment I host for *NW Prime Time* Sharing Stories at http://northwestprimetime.com/ LOCAL page, Sharing Stories. Send your stories or poems to me at ariele@comcast.net. My columns Writing Corner and Poetry Corner are in the print version of *NW Prime Time* which is free at libraries and senior centers in the Seattle area.
I teach onsite writing classes in the Seattle area and online classes to people all over the world. Email me for a complete list of class titles.
ariele@comcast.net

Amazon.com eBooks by Ariele M. Huff

Making Mud Angels: Winning Strategies in Tough Times
Need a fresh start? Help is here. Achieve success when finances, diet, health, or relationships are troubled. Easy Action Plans are gifts from tried and true wisdoms of the ages. Join the fun path to a better life.
KITTEN LOVE: Three kittens in a box under a bush. What was I to do but take them home? In this game changing choice, I've learned a lot about myself, my husband, our two elderly pets, and how a single moment can make your life over--whether you wanted that or not! A raucous ride with melting moments and adorable photos. Plus, a couple of bumbling pet owners hoping to survive their best intentions. HELP!
Learn from My Mistakes An open diary of the happy, healing, humorous adventure—exploring obstacles & discovering solutions—bringing three abandoned kittens into our lives!
Crazy Cat Ladies and why we do that This is the story of how my husband and I graduated from lifetime owners of one-cat-at-a-time to Crazy Cat Ladies and why we love it so much. The answer is NOT what you think it is!
Fifty Shades of Graying: Love, Romance, and Sex After Fifty The result of a blog where people shared stories, essays, & poems on the topic.
The Perks of Aging: Blessings, Silver Linings, & Convenient Half-Truths Road map to happier golden years, often given as a gift. The lists of perks in elder decades are from a group of people over fifty. The short poems are lighthearted & thought-provoking. Join the hundreds who have valued this inexpensive little book in navigating the third age—with a sense of humor & joy.

Made in the USA
Middletown, DE
11 May 2015